C902125080

KT-147-249

LIBRARIES NI
WITHDRAWN FROM STOCK

Daisy Doodles

For Michelle and Daisy x MR
For my parents, who always supported my doodling, with love. ID
For Thea and Samson—keep doodling, you never know where it might take you. TW

OXFORD
UNIVERSITY PRESS

Great Clarendon Street, Oxford OX2 6DP

Oxford University Press is a department of the University of Oxford.
It furthers the University's objective of excellence in research, scholarship,
and education by publishing worldwide. Oxford is a registered trade mark of
Oxford University Press in the UK and in certain other countries

Text copyright © Michelle Robinson 2017
Illustration copyright © Irene Dickson 2017
Photography copyright © Oxford University Press 2017

The moral rights of the author and artist have been asserted

Database right Oxford University Press (maker)

First published 2017

All rights reserved. No part of this publication may be reproduced,
stored in a retrieval system, or transmitted, in any form or by any means,
without the prior permission in writing of Oxford University Press,
or as expressly permitted by law, or under terms agreed with the appropriate
reprographics rights organization. Enquiries concerning reproduction
outside the scope of the above should be sent to the Rights Department,
Oxford University Press, at the address above.

You must not circulate this book in any other binding or cover
and you must impose this same condition on any acquirer

British Library Cataloguing in Publication Data available

ISBN: 978-0-19-274867-6 (paperback)
ISBN: 978-0-19-274868-3 (ebook)

1 3 5 7 9 10 8 6 4 2

Printed in China

Paper used in the production of this book is a natural, recyclable product made
from wood grown in sustainable forests. The manufacturing process conforms
to the environmental regulations of the country of origin

The publisher would like to thank Lara, Phoebe, and Kristina
for their assistance, stellar performance, and warm hospitality.

Daisy Doodles

Michelle Robinson

Irene Dickson

Tom Weller

OXFORD
UNIVERSITY PRESS

It was raining. Again.

Even the cat was staying indoors.

Daisy was drawing a picture.

Daisy gave him a name.

PiPSqueak

And added just one more whisker.

But as Daisy doodled . . .

'Aaa . . . .

'Aaa . . . .

'Aaa . . . .

'Aaaa-TISH-oooo!'

Pipsqueak sneezed himself
right off the page!

Daisy dropped her pencil.
Pipsqueak grabbed it.

'Please?'
he said.

Well, he did ask nicely . . .

And he was *very*
good at drawing.

Soon they were sticking stars on the sofa.

Fishes on the floor.

Monkeys on the mantelpiece.

The whole place
was decorated
with doodles.

'Ready?'
said Pipsqueak.

'Ready for what?'
said Daisy.

'Wonderful things,'
said Pipsqueak.
'Follow Me.'

Then the rain had gone,
and the room had gone too!

They drew dragons
and dragonflies . . .

. . . coloured castles
and carousels.

Made up mermaids
and shaded in ships.

Daisy thought it might
be even more fun
if the cat joined in.

NOT a good idea!

And so it began.

THE BATTLE OF CRAYON CREEK

Look out,
Pipsqueak!

There were PAWS and CLAWS . . .

and JAWS . . .

and ROARS . . .

All that noise woke up the *tickly* octopus, who chased them all back home!

'Oh, Daisy!' said mum.
'You scared the cat.'

'We were just playing,'
said Daisy.
'Tell her, Pipsqueak.'

But Pipsqueak didn't even
wiggle a whisker . . .

'Come on,' Mum said gently.
'Let's clean all this up. It'll be quicker if we do it together.'

Pencils in pots.

Craft things in tins.

Pictures put safely away.

By the time everything
had been tidied up,
it had stopped raining

'I think you're ready for a
new doodle pad,' said Mum.
'And don't forget to eat your cookie,
before a little mouse gets it!'

But Daisy thought maybe a little mouse *should* get the cookie.

She left it with a note, for Pipsqueak, just in case he should come back.

You never know, he just might . . .